MONSTERS DON'T READ

HEATHER CHAMPION ILLUSTRATED BY CHRIS KNUDSON

Monsters Don't Read
ISBN: 978-0-9819591-1-5

Copyright © 2010 Heather Champion
Illustrations by Chris Knudson

Bronze Man Books
Millikin University
1184 W. Main
Decatur, IL 62522
www.bronzemanbooks.com

To Jesse, my husband, and Clover, our own little **monster**, for listening to this story 1000 times without complaining. Also, to Mom and Dad who always read to me, especially the **monster** books.

This year my class learns to read.

My teacher writes the ABCs,

The class spells words like C-A-T,

But...

I am a **monster** and **monsters** don't read.

2

Each day we have story time,

And we learn lots of rhymes.

But, I will not learn to read,

No matter how much fun it seems.

3

4

My teacher puts words on the wall.

She reads out loud and stands up tall.

I hope she won't call on me,

Because...

I am a **monster** and **monsters** don't read.

6

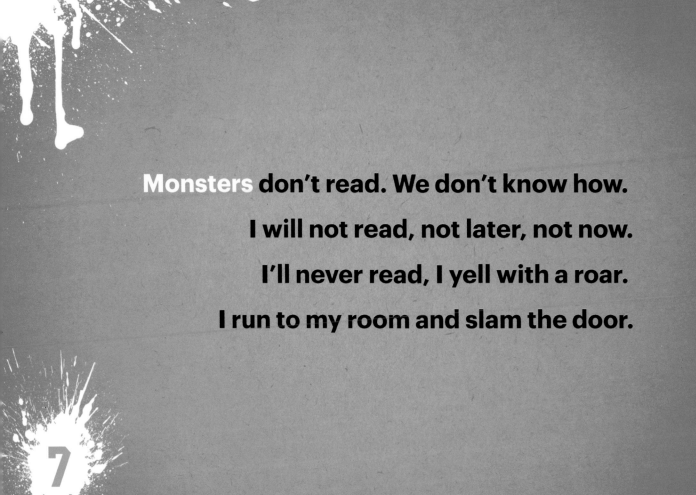

Monsters don't read. We don't know how.

I will not read, not later, not now.

I'll never read, I yell with a roar.

I run to my room and slam the door.

7

8

The words don't make sense in my head.

Reading makes my face turn red.

So I will not read you see,

My friends might all make fun of me.

11

During class I sit in back

And hide my face in my lunch sack.

My classmates read books about knights and fairies.

Me? I just think books are scary!

Reading will never be fun.

A reader? I'll never be one.

Books are not the thing for me

Because...

I am a **monster** and **monsters**

don't read.

14

My whole class reads, except for me.

And they all just let me be.

While everyone reads I'm on my own.

It's not fun playing all alone.

15

16

Then one day at the library I see

A book on the shelf featuring me!

A monster book where monsters rule?

How could a book be so cool?

18

I look around, I have to sneak.

When no one's looking I take a peek.

Every page is a surprise.

I see some words I recognize!

20

Each picture is bright and bold.

Reading this book would never get old.

With each new turn stories unfold.

If I can't read, it goes untold.

This is a book I cannot pass.

Finally I can play with my class.

I check out the book, and take it home.

I want to read all on my own.

24

Reading is hard, but I want to know how.

I'm scared to read... but I have to know NOW!

My teacher says she will help me.

Maybe...

I am a monster and monsters can read.

26

So I learn my ABCs,

And I spell out C-A-T.

I learn the vowels A, E, I, O, U.

I practice small words, big ones too!

I learn rhymes like fine and pine.

I sit and listen during story time.

My teacher says it's time for me

To try it on my own, to read!

I can read my book out loud.

All my friends are really proud!

They smile, cheer, and clap for me,

Now

I am a monster and I can read!

33

I can read books with my class.

I read through them really fast.

Each day I read with ease.

I love to read. You can't stop me!

34

I'm not afraid to read at school.

I think reading is really cool.

I read in the closet, I read at night.

I read in trees, it's quite a sight.

35

I read out loud and in my head,

I even read under my bed.

I read on the stairs, I read in the hall.

There is no place I won't read at all.

38

39

Reading is my favorite thing.

Because...

I am a **monster** and **monsters** do read!

For **Heather Champion** Monsters Don't Read grew out of early literacy experiences, reading with her father, and her work in the field of Early Childhood Education. Heather recently graduated from Millikin University with a degree in Early Childhood Education and is currently teaching a second grade class at Argenta-Oreana Elementary School where she inspires her own students to never be afraid to try.

Chris Knudson is a graphic designer with a passion for illustration. Chris graduated from Millikin University in 2010 with a degree in Commercial Art. He worked with Bronze Man Books for five years and now runs his design business Energetic Aesthetic. He would like to thank Heather for the opportunity to bring her story to life.